Superhero Superstars

Jason Momoa

by Martha London

FOCUS READERS

BEACON

www.focusreaders.com

Focus Readers is distributed by North Star Editions:
sales@northstareditions.com | 888-417-0195

Produced for Focus Readers by Red Line Editorial.

Photographs ©: Jordan Strauss/Invision/AP Images, cover, 1; DC Comics/DN Entertainment/Warner Bros/Album/Newscom, 4, 6, 25, 29; Shutterstock Images, 8, 17, 18, 22, 26; Jim Ruymen/UPI/Newscom, 11; Sony Pictures Television/ACME Shark/MGM Television Pegasus/Album/Newscom, 12; Hollyn Johnson/Hawaii Tribune-Herald/AP Images, 14; Warner Bros./Photofest, 20–21

Library of Congress Cataloging-in-Publication Data
Names: London, Martha, author.
Title: Jason Momoa / by Martha London.
Description: Lake Elmo, MN : Focus Readers, [2021] | Series: Superhero superstars | Includes index. | Audience: Grades: 4-6
Identifiers: LCCN 2020004010 (print) | LCCN 2020004011 (ebook) | ISBN 9781644933732 (hardcover) | ISBN 9781644934494 (paperback) | ISBN 9781644936016 (pdf) | ISBN 9781644935255 (ebook)
Subjects: LCSH: Momoa, Jason--Juvenile literature. | Motion picture actors and actresses--United States--Biography--Juvenile literature. | Television actors and actresses--United States--Biography--Juvenile literature.
Classification: LCC PN2287.M658 L66 2021 (print) | LCC PN2287.M658 (ebook) | DDC 791.43092 [B]--dc23
LC record available at https://lccn.loc.gov/2020004010
LC ebook record available at https://lccn.loc.gov/2020004011

Printed in the United States of America
Mankato, MN
082020

About the Author

Martha London writes books for young readers full-time. When she isn't writing, she can be found hiking in the woods.

Table of Contents

Chapter 1

Aquaman

Aquaman and Mera run across the roofs of houses. They dodge lasers. The sounds of explosions echo in the air. A **villain** is after them. Mera jumps from one roof. Aquaman jumps from another.

Aquaman is often seen carrying the Trident of Neptune, a powerful magic weapon.

Aquaman's friend Mera has the power to control water around her.

They crash to the floor of a house. Aquaman looks up and grins.

Jason Momoa stands up. He looks around at the cameras. He

helps his costar up. Momoa plays Aquaman. The **director** walks over to the actors. The actors listen to his instructions. Momoa cracks a joke. The director laughs. Momoa and his costar walk back to their starting places. They go through the scene again.

Fun Fact

***Aquaman* is based on a comic book. In one version of the comic, Aquaman was raised by dolphins.**

Chapter 2

Early Life

Jason Momoa was born on August 1, 1979, in Honolulu, Hawaii. Momoa is **biracial**. His father is Hawaiian and works as a painter. His mother is white and works as a photographer.

Momoa and his family attend the first showing of *Aquaman* in 2018.

Jason did not grow up in Hawaii. He moved to Iowa as a child. His mother raised him there by herself. Jason was active as a child. He played many sports.

Momoa started college in Iowa. He studied wildlife **biology**. Momoa loved what he was studying. He

Fun Fact

The haka is a dance of the Maori people of New Zealand. It spread to Hawaii. Momoa learned it from his father.

Momoa performed the haka dance when *Aquaman* first played in Hollywood.

cares about nature. But he also wanted to be more active. Momoa decided not to finish his college degree.

Instead, Momoa moved back to Hawaii. He started modeling.

Momoa played Ronon Dex in *Stargate: Atlantis*. The show is about soldiers in space.

When he was 20, he got his first acting **role**. Momoa played a lifeguard on a TV show.

Momoa hoped the role would lead to other acting opportunities. But he had trouble getting other parts. Directors did not take his lifeguard role seriously. So, they did not take Momoa seriously. He only got a few small roles. Eventually, Momoa was cast in the television series *Stargate: Atlantis*. It was the break he was looking for. Momoa's acting career took off after that.

Fun Fact

Momoa worked in a T-shirt shop before he got his first acting role.

Chapter 3

Helping Earth

Momoa is tall and strong. He plays a lot of action characters. His characters are often fighters. For this reason, many people do not think Momoa is kind. They think he is like the characters he plays.

Momoa's children sometimes join him when he takes action to help the planet.

But Momoa is more than just a fighter. People who know him say he is funny. He also loves the outdoors. He works hard to help the planet.

For example, Momoa is tackling the issue of plastic bottles. People often use plastic bottles

Fun Fact

Momoa enjoys outdoor sports. He likes rock climbing and surfing. He also goes mountain biking and snowboarding.

In 2017, 26.8 tons (24.3 metric tons) of plastic waste was sent to landfills.

for drinking water. But plastic is wasteful. People throw it away. The plastic gets sent to landfills. There, it lasts a very long time.

Momoa cares about the environment. He also speaks out against climate change.

Rain can wash plastic into the ocean. The plastic breaks down into tiny pieces. Fish and other animals eat the pieces. The plastic pieces hurt them.

Momoa is trying to help fix this problem. He works with a company that uses aluminum cans instead of plastic bottles for holding water. Aluminum is easier to **recycle** than plastic.

Momoa wants to protect the planet. But he knows that everyone has to do his or her part. Momoa tries to make it easier for people to help Earth and the environment.

Blue Screens

Much of *Aquaman* takes place underwater. But the actors did not film the movie underwater. Instead, they used a blue screen. It took the place of the **set**. Actors said their lines in front of the screen. They could not see an underwater world around them. They had to pretend they were underwater.

Later, artists used computers to create the background. They replaced the blue screen with images of fish, buildings, and dark water. These images made it look like the characters were in the ocean.

Aquaman can swim and breathe underwater.

Chapter 4

Breaking New Ground

In the comics, Aquaman is white and has blond hair. But Momoa is biracial. *Aquaman*'s **producers** still knew Momoa was right for the role. The character is half Atlantean and half white.

Momoa attends the first showing of *Justice League* in 2017.

Momoa used his experiences as a biracial person to know how Aquaman feels in the movie. Momoa also played Aquaman in *Justice League*. He made Aquaman one of the first biracial superheroes to appear in a live-action movie.

Momoa has always had an active lifestyle. But he still had to prepare

Fun Fact

Momoa likes to play his guitar in between filming scenes.

Aquaman often uses his water powers when he fights against enemies.

for the role of Aquaman. Aquaman is a strong fighter, so Momoa learned different fighting styles. He also lifted weights and changed what he ate. Momoa wanted his acting to be believable.

Momoa poses with his costars at the first showing of *Justice League* in 2017.

The *Aquaman* movie had a fight **choreographer**. This person designed the movie's fight scenes. Each actor has different strengths. Some actors are small and fast.

Momoa is tall and strong. The choreographer chose different moves for him than for other actors. For example, Aquaman can lift his enemies. He can throw them across a room.

Momoa has his own movie company. He works as an actor, writer, director, and producer. After *Aquaman*, Momoa wrote and produced a series of short movies. Momoa also planned to return as Aquaman in future films.

FOCUS ON

Jason Momoa

Write your answers on a separate piece of paper.

1. Write a paragraph summarizing the main ideas of Chapter 3.
2. Why do you think it's important for biracial superheroes to appear in movies?
3. How did filmmakers create the underwater world in *Aquaman*?
   - **A.** They filmed underwater.
   - **B.** They used a blue screen.
   - **C.** They went to Atlantis.
4. Why might Momoa continue to get cast as fighters or action characters?
   - **A.** He cares about the planet.
   - **B.** He is good at acting in front of blue screens.
   - **C.** He is tall and strong, like a fighter.

5. What does **tackling** mean in this book?

*He works hard to help the planet. For example, Momoa is **tackling** the issue of plastic bottles.*

A. making sure people use an object

B. knocking other people to the ground

C. working to deal with a problem

6. What does **break** mean in this book?

*It was the **break** he was looking for. Momoa's acting career took off after that.*

A. a bit of luck

B. a broken bone

C. a worse job

Answer key on page 32.

Glossary

biology
The study of living things.

biracial
Having parents from two different races.

choreographer
A person who creates dance or fight routines.

director
A person who is in charge of making a movie.

producers
People who find money to pay for the filming of a movie.

recycle
To take apart an old item and make the pieces into something new.

role
The part an actor plays in a television show or movie.

set
A collection of furniture, objects, and backgrounds used for a particular scene of a movie.

villain
A character who works against the hero of a story.

To Learn More

BOOKS

Hammelef, Danielle S. *Behind-the-Scenes Movie Careers.* North Mankato, MN: Capstone Press, 2017.

Scott, Melanie. *DC Ultimate Character Guide.* New York: DK Publishing, 2019.

Summers, Portia. *Was Atlantis Real?* New York: Enslow Publishing, 2018.

NOTE TO EDUCATORS

Visit **www.focusreaders.com** to find lesson plans, activities, links, and other resources related to this title.

Index

Answer Key: 1. Answers will vary; **2.** Answers will vary; **3.** B; **4.** C; **5.** C; **6.** A